I Wonder
How Parrots Can Talk

and other neat facts about birds

By Mary Packard
Illustrated by Robin Brickman

A GOLDEN BOOK • NEW YORK
Western Publishing Company, Inc., Racine, Wisconsin 53404

Produced by Graymont Enterprises, Inc., Norfolk, Connecticut
Producer: *Ruth Lerner Perle*
Design: *Michele Italiano-Perla*
Editorial consultant: *Robert Sweet*, American Museum of Natural History, New York

Contents

What does it take to be a bird?

There are thousands and thousands of different kinds of birds living on our planet. They come in many different sizes and colors, they live in different places, and they have different habits. But all birds have some things in common that make them birds and not anything else.

A bird must have:

Feathers
All birds have feathers. Even the tiniest hummingbird has more than a thousand.

A beak
Birds have hard beaks that help them gather food, tidy their feathers, and build nests.

Wings
All birds have two wings, but not all birds can fly.

Two legs
Birds have two legs. Their feet usually have four toes—one usually points backward.

One or more songs
All birds sing or call. Some know only one song. Others can sing dozens.

Eggs
All birds lay eggs. Most adult birds sit on the eggs until the baby birds hatch.

Warm blood
Birds have a high body temperature that remains the same no matter what the outside temperature may be.

4

Why is a bat not a bird?

Bats have wings but not feathers. Their bodies are covered with fur. Baby bats drink mother's milk.

Why is a butterfly not a bird?

Butterflies have four wings, six legs, and they don't have feathers. Like all insects, they have an outer covering, or *exoskeleton*, but they don't have bones. Butterflies do lay eggs, but they don't care for them the way most birds do. Butterflies don't have beaks, and they don't sing.

What are feathers?

Feathers are made of the same lightweight, bendable material that human hair and nails are made of.

The outer feathers, or *contour* feathers, are smooth and stiff and give the bird its shape. The wing contour feathers are the longest and are specially designed for steering the bird as it flies. The tail contour feathers are the widest and are perfect for giving the bird balance. Contour feathers are like an overcoat. They keep warmth in and water out.

Beneath the contour feathers are the soft and fluffy *down* feathers. They are close to the bird's body, acting like a soft blanket to keep it cozy and warm.

Amazing *but* TRUE

A kiwi's wings, only two inches long, are useless. Its feathers are unusual because they look more like hair.

How do birds build nests?

Not all birds build nests, but those that do must first find a place that is safe and protected from animals that eat eggs and baby birds. Birds often scout for the perfect spot for days before they start building. Usually the male and female work together to make a strong, cozy nest that will hold the eggs and later the baby chicks.

Do all nests look alike?

Every kind of bird builds a different kind of nest. They come in many shapes and sizes. A bald eagle's nest can weigh as much as two tons, while a hummingbird's nest is not much bigger than a thimble and weighs a few ounces.

Cave swiftlets make their nests entirely out of saliva. When nesting season is over, people collect the nests and use them to make a popular Chinese delicacy known as "bird's-nest soup."

A robin's nest

1 Robins start building by gathering small twigs for the main part of their nests. If they live near people's houses, they might find bits of foil, string, cotton, or yarn and add them to the nest.

2 Using their feet and beaks, the robins bend the twigs into the shape of a cup. Then they make an inner wall out of mud. Next, they line the nest with leaves and any other soft things they can find.

Amazing *but* TRUE

When the outside of a duck's nest is complete, the female often plucks the soft feathers from her breast and uses the down to line the nest.

3 When the nest is dry and comfortable, the female lays her eggs.

Stitchers

Tailorbirds use their beaks to punch holes around the edges of a leaf. Then they poke pieces of grass through the holes, making a cozy pocket for the nest.

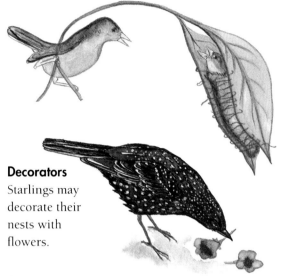

Decorators

Starlings may decorate their nests with flowers.

Apartment owners

Weaverbirds use dried grass or straw to weave one big hanging nest for the whole flock. Then each pair of birds makes a tunnel to get to its own "room."

Wall builders

Most hornbills make their nests in tree hollows. As soon as the female climbs into the hole to lay her eggs, the male fills the entrance with mud to make a wall. He leaves a tiny opening so he can pass food to her until the baby birds hatch.

Borrowers and takers

Some puffins lay their eggs in rabbit holes. Cuckoos just drop their eggs in the nests of other birds.

Do birds have 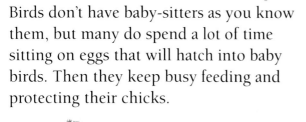 baby-sitters?

Birds don't have baby-sitters as you know them, but many do spend a lot of time sitting on eggs that will hatch into baby birds. Then they keep busy feeding and protecting their chicks.

How long do birds sit on their nests?

Once the mother bird has laid her eggs, she has the job of keeping them at the right temperature so that they will hatch. She does this by gently covering the eggs with her body until the baby birds (inside the eggs) break out of their shells. This can take anywhere from ten to eighty days. While they are sitting on their nests, most birds turn their eggs over every few days so that the chicks inside won't get stuck to one side of their shells.

How do chicks get out of their shells?

Many baby chicks have a special *egg tooth* to help them peck their way out of their shells. The egg tooth, which is the only tooth a bird ever has, falls off soon after the little chick has hatched.

How do parent birds take care of their new babies?

For the first few days of their lives, the newborn birds need to eat more than their body weight to survive. Many parent birds spend most of their time bringing food to their babies. Baby turkeys, chickens, and waterfowl, such as ducks, can feed themselves as soon as they hatch.

Amazing *but* TRUE

The sandgrouse lives in the desert, where water is hard to find. He flies as far as fifty miles to find water for his babies. When he gets to a watering hole, he soaks his spongelike breast feathers. Then he flies back to his family, who drink from his water-soaked feathers.

Tell Me More

The male finfoot, also known as the sun-grebe, carries his chicks in special pockets under his wings. That way, he can even fly with them.

9

How do birds learn to fly?

Birds don't have to take flying lessons. They know how to fly from the moment they are born. But they don't fly out of the nest until they have more feathers and their wings are stronger. Most baby birds start to flutter their wings when they are only a few days old.

When the young *fledglings* are finally ready to leave the nest, the mother flies out, and they follow her one at a time. Sometimes a timid bird has to be coaxed out of the nest by its mother. Then the mother perches on the branch of a nearby tree, holding food in her mouth. That's usually all it takes for the young one to jump out of the nest and try its wings.

Do all birds eat worms?

Different birds eat different kinds of food. A hungry little robin might satisfy its appetite with a worm, but a big bird, like an eagle, needs a heartier meal to fill its stomach. The shape of a bird's beak, or *bill*, is a good clue to what it eats. Beaks may be large or small. They may be shaped like tweezers, spoons, shovels, knives, cones, or nutcrackers.

Nectar sippers
A hummingbird's needlelike beak is perfect for reaching the sweet liquid, or *nectar*, deep inside a flower.

Hunters
Eagles and other meat eaters hunt for animals. Hooks on their beaks help them tear food apart.

Fishers
Many fishing birds, like loons, have beaks that open wide. These birds swallow their catch whole.

Drillers
To find its favorite bugs, the woodpecker uses its long, thick beak to drill holes into the bark of trees.

Seed pickers
Finches and other birds that eat seeds have short, cone-shaped beaks. These are perfect for picking seeds and cracking them open.

Strainers
A flamingo eats snails and shrimp that are mixed in the mud at the bottom of ponds. When it scoops up a beakful of mud, it uses its tongue to push mud out through the slits in its beak so that the food gets trapped in its mouth.

Fruit eaters
Fruit eaters, like toucans, have lobster claw–shaped beaks with saw-toothed edges for tearing fruit from trees and then cutting it into chunks.

Amazing *but* TRUE

Oxpeckers are little gray birds with bright-red beaks. They ride on the backs of oxen, rhinoceroses, and other big animals. Using their tweezerlike beaks, they clean fleas and ticks from the animals' hides.

Why are male birds often more colorful than females?

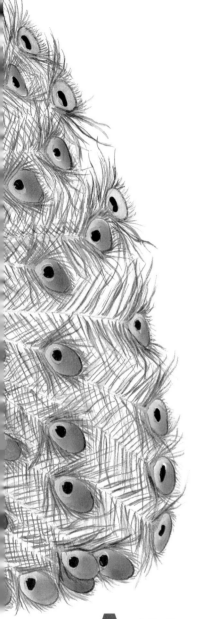

It seems strange that most male birds have spectacular feathers or plumage, but that most females are drab. Like most things in nature, however, there is a good reason for this. Since the female is usually the one who sits on the nest, it's important for her feathers to blend in with her surroundings so that no one will disturb her. If she had brighter feathers, her enemies would spot her easily and try to get her eggs or chicks.

The male uses his brightly colored feathers to attract females and scare off other males. He has to convince the female of his choice that he's special and worthy of her attention. So he struts back and forth before her, showing off his fancy feathers. Every bird has a different way of displaying his feathers.
• The peacock flirts by raising his tail feathers to create a magnificent fan.
• The night heron shakes his head back and forth, stamps his feet in place, and sings a special song.
• The bird of paradise hangs upside down so that the female can see the beautiful feathers under his tail.

Amazing but TRUE

In addition to attracting a female with his feathers and songs, the male Australian bowerbird builds her a house out of twigs and decorates it with shells, berries, pebbles, and flowers. When the flowers wilt, he replaces them with fresh ones.

Tell Me More

A male peacock's feathers have a pattern of colorful circles that look very much like eyes. This pattern is not only beautiful but also useful. If a peacock sees an enemy approaching, he raises his feathers. When the enemy sees all those staring "eyes," it often gets scared and runs away.

Why do SWANS have such long necks?

Swans gliding smoothly on a pond or lake are a beautiful sight. With their long, graceful necks held high, they look like kings and queens ruling over the other water birds. But swans' necks are not just for looking beautiful. Swans need their long necks to reach for the underwater plants they love to eat.

Why is a swan's neck so curvy?

A swan has twenty-five bones in its neck. All those bones make it possible for a swan to twist its neck in almost any direction. The only time a swan keeps its long neck perfectly straight is when it is flying.

How do swans glide on the water?

The toes of most water birds, such as swans, ducks, and geese, are connected by flaps of skin called *webs*. Water birds use their webbed feet to paddle through the water the way you would use oars with a rowboat. Since they do their paddling below the water, they don't splash or ripple the surface.

All in the family

Like most waterfowl babies, swan chicks, or *cygnets*, are born knowing how to swim. Almost as soon as they hatch, they line up in the water and start to paddle. The male swan, called a *cob*, leads the way to make sure there is no danger ahead. The female, called a *pen*, swims at the end of the line so that she can keep an eye on each precious chick. Sometimes a chick will get tired. When this happens, the mother swims over to it and raises one webbed foot. The chick then steps onto its mother's foot and climbs on her back for a ride.

Amazing but TRUE

When a swan chick hatches, it follows the first moving thing it sees. If, for some reason, its mother isn't there, it will follow any other animal—a duck, a dog, a cat, or even a person!

Why don't water birds' feathers get soaked?

When a bird *preens*, or cleans and arranges its feathers, it waterproofs them at the same time. It presses on a gland at the base of its tail, and a special oily substance escapes onto its bill. The bird then rubs its oily bill on its feathers. When water comes in contact with the oily feathers, it forms little beads and rolls right off.

15

Why does the ostrich hide its head?

Some people think that an ostrich buries its head in the sand when it is frightened. This is a tall tale about a tall bird! The story may have begun because the female has a special way of protecting her eggs. When she senses danger, she covers the eggs with her body, lowers her head, and rests it on the ground. That way she looks more like a great big thornbush than an ostrich, and an enemy might not notice her.

Why can't the ostrich fly?

The ostrich is the largest bird on earth. It grows taller than the tallest human being—seven to eight feet tall—and it can weigh more than three hundred pounds. Although it has wings, the ostrich is too big and heavy to fly. But it has other ways of making a fast getaway.

How does the ostrich defend itself?

Ostriches are among the fastest runners on earth and can outrun most of their enemies. Ostriches can run up to sixty miles an hour. That's faster than most birds can fly. They are great kickers, too. If a hungry predator gets too close, it had better watch out! One kick from the ostrich's powerful leg can send an animal hurtling through the air.

The great pretenders

Ostriches are fine actors, and they use their talent to protect their chicks. When an ostrich sees a lion or other enemy coming, it screeches out and pretends that it has a broken leg. The lion, thinking that the ostrich is unable to defend itself, comes closer to get a better look. That's when the ostrich delivers a swift, sharp kick.

The ostrich lays the world's biggest egg. It is about six inches long, four inches wide, and weighs about three pounds. That's equal to eighteen chicken eggs, or about fifty robin eggs. Pictured here, for comparison, not actual size, are the eggs of the ostrich, chicken, robin, and hummingbird, which is the smallest egg—about the size of a pea.

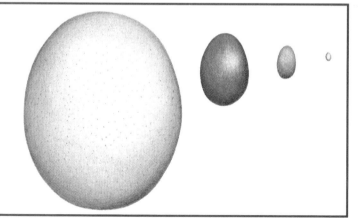

Tell Me More

Ostrich parents take turns sitting on their nest. The female has brown feathers that blend in perfectly with the desert sand, and so she guards the nest in the daytime. The male ostrich has a mixture of shiny black feathers and curly white plumes. His feathers are easy to see in the daytime, but at night they appear to be shadows and can barely be seen. So the male guards the nest at night.

Amazing but TRUE

Sometimes ostriches travel with herds of warthogs or zebras. As the animals stomp through the grass and sand, they kick up insects that ostriches like to eat. In return, the tall birds, which can see farther than the shorter animals, warn their hosts when they spot an enemy in the distance.

Why do birds sing?

Birds sing to send messages to other birds or animals, to show off, and to protect their nests. Sometimes they sing just for the fun of it. Some of their sounds are only one-note calls. But whether they are singing or calling, all the sounds birds make have special meaning, and they have different songs for different occasions.

Love songs

Chances are, if you hear a bird singing, the bird is a male. A male bird sings his most beautiful songs to make himself seem special to females. If a female likes what she hears, she will make a nest with him!

Home-sweet-home songs

When two birds have found just the right place to build their home, they sing a song that warns other birds to stay away from their nest and the area around it. The song might sound like a beautiful lullaby to us, but what it is really saying is: "This nest is ours. Stay away!"

S.O.S. songs

Birds call out to warn other birds or animals that danger is near. Their signals are a matter of life or death to those listening for them. Birds have different warnings for different dangers. One call may mean: "Look out! Here comes a fox!" Another: "Take cover. A hawk is overhead!" Even before they hatch, birds inside their shells suddenly become silent when a parent sends its danger call.

How do birds learn to sing?

Baby birds start practicing their songs when they are just a few days old. This baby talk, or *sub-song*, is sung with beaks closed, and sounds a bit like humming. All birds learn to sing from their parents. If a baby oriole is separated from its parents at birth and never gets to hear other orioles singing, it will never sing exactly like an oriole.

Do nightingales sing only at night?

Nightingales sing beautiful songs, both by day and by night. But their songs are heard best at night, when most other birds are silent.

Tell Me More

Each kind of bird has its own special song. All cardinals sing the same warning song, but their warning song is different from the one that blue jays sing.

Amazing
but TRUE

Most storks can make only low grunts and hisses. They communicate by making a noisy, clattering sound with their beaks.

Are owls really wise?

Owls look as if they see all and know all. That's because their huge round eyes face front, like human eyes, instead of sideways, like other birds' eyes. An owl's steady stare makes it look very wise, but it really is no wiser than any other bird. Owls are great hunters, however.

Why do owls hunt?

Owls are *carnivores*. That means they eat meat, and so they must hunt for small prey such as mice, skunks, or snakes.

See all

Most owls do their hunting at night, and they are perfectly equipped for the job because they can see better in the dark than people can in daylight. Not only do owls have wonderful sight, but they can swivel their heads almost all the way around. Thus they can see things behind their backs.

Hear all

Even though owls' ears are covered with feathers, their hearing is so sharp that they can pick up even the slightest sound. Each ear has two flaps that face both forward and backward, so the owl can hear equally well in all directions. An owl can tell exactly where a squeaking mouse is hiding just by swiveling its head and moving its earflaps.

Catch all

Another reason owls make such good hunters is that other animals can't hear them coming. Most birds make a lot of noise when they flap their wings. But not owls. The edges of an owl's flight feathers are looser and softer than those of other birds. So when they swoop down to catch their prey, they can do it in silence.

Amazing but TRUE

Burrowing owls live in underground tunnels and they have a special way of getting rid of unwelcome visitors. Anyone poking around their home will be surprised by a very scary sound. That's because these owls know just how to copy the sound that a rattlesnake makes.

Do all birds live in trees?

Most birds spend their lives flying among the branches of trees in woods and forests. Trees are a good source of food—insects, nuts, fruits, and berries. Their leafy branches provide shade, protection from bad weather, and escape from predators that like birds for dinner. Some birds, however, live in sandy deserts or on rocky mountaintops that have no trees. Others live near the water, and still others make their homes on city buildings.

Rooftops
Storks often make their nests on country-house rooftops. In Holland, France, and Belgium, people believe it is good luck to have storks nesting on the roof.

22

Cactus caves

There are no trees in the desert, so the Gila woodpecker carves its nest into giant saguaro cacti. When the woodpecker moves out of its hole, the elf owl moves in to raise its family.

Waterside

Water birds, like ducks, swans, and geese, live close to the water and establish their homes among the reeds there.

How do homing pigeons find their way home?

No matter where they start out, trained homing pigeons always come home—even from places they've never been before. Nobody knows just how this amazing inborn talent, or *instinct,* works. Scientists do know that pigeons don't use their eyes to find their way. To prove this, they fitted clouded contact lenses on some pigeons' eyes so they couldn't see where they were going. Still, the pigeons had no trouble finding their way home.

How do people train pigeons?

A pigeon trainer keeps twenty or thirty young pigeons on a rooftop and takes good care of them. Every day, the trainer shoos the pigeons off the roof, and when they come back, they are rewarded with food. Each day, the pigeons fly farther and farther from the roof, but they always come back for their treat. Once a pigeon is trained, its owner can take it miles away, but when it is released, it will always fly back to its rooftop home.

How do pigeons carry messages?

Homing pigeons have been useful for carrying important information from faraway places back to their owners. A message is written on a small strip of paper and inserted in a tiny tube that is attached to the pigeon's leg. When the bird arrives at its destination, the tube is removed and the message can be read.

Amazing *but* TRUE

In ancient Rome, long before there were telephones, radios, or fax machines, a famous emperor named Julius Caesar used pigeons to bring him news from all parts of his huge empire. He had human messengers, too, but none were as quick and reliable as the pigeons.

How can parrots talk?

Parrots have an amazing ability to copy the sounds that people make, but nobody knows how they do it. Some scientists believe that parrots talk because they need to feel a close bond or friendship with another creature. One way they make this bond is by copying the sounds that the other creature makes. Wild parrots copy the calls of other parrots, but when parrots are around people, they imitate the sounds people make.

Do parrots understand what they say?

Most scientists think that though parrots repeat words, they don't know what those words mean. Sometimes a parrot will figure out the right time to say a word. It might say "Come in" when someone knocks on the door, or "Hello" when the telephone rings. Does a parrot understand what it is saying? Only the parrot knows for sure.

Table manners

Parrots are like people in another way. Most birds stand on both feet and peck at their food with their beaks. But the parrot feeds itself by taking food in its foot and bringing it to its mouth—pretty much the way you use your hand to bring a sandwich to your mouth. Some parrots are right-footed and others are left-footed. A left-footed parrot always feeds itself with its left foot.

Tell Me More

Instead of oil, parrots produce a special cleaning powder to keep their feathers clean and groomed.

How do penguins keep warm?

Most penguins live in Antarctica, which is near the South Pole, one of the coldest regions on our planet. But these penguins seem to like the cold and ice. They have a thick layer of fat that acts like a blanket and keeps them nice and warm on the coldest day. On top of the fat, penguins have three layers of short, oily feathers. These feathers are like a second blanket, keeping the heat in and the cold out.

When the icy polar wind is blowing hard, as many as five thousand penguins huddle together in a circle to protect themselves from the cold.

Why can't penguins fly?

Penguins don't know how to fly, and they don't walk too well, either. They can slide and toboggan on the ice, and some can hop. But when it comes to swimming, they are wonderfully swift and graceful. That's because penguins use their wings like flippers to glide through the water with ease. Emperor penguins can dive deep into the water and stay down for almost twenty minutes.

Amazing *but* TRUE

Emperor penguin parents share the job of caring for their chicks. The female lays one egg on the ice and goes off to feed in warmer waters. The male then rolls the egg onto his webbed feet and covers it with a flap of skin under his belly. He stands that way in the cold for two months without eating until the egg hatches. Then the female returns and the male goes off to feed.

How do pelicans catch fish?

Pelicans are among the largest birds on earth, and they are one of nature's great fishers. The leathery pouch under their big beak works like a built-in fishing net.

When the pelican goes fishing, it dips its wide-open beak into the sea and fills its pouch with many gallons of water. Then the pelican snaps its beak shut and tips it forward to drain all the water out. What's left is a mouthful of fish, which the pelican then swallows in one gulp. When a pelican is not eating, its pouch folds under its beak like an umbrella.

Pelican islands

When it's time to lay eggs and hatch babies, pelicans get together and take over whole islands just for themselves. Many of these islands are named Pelican Island in honor of their feathered guests. There are Pelican islands in Canada, Australia, Africa, and the United States. When other birds flock together, they are usually a very noisy lot. But not pelicans. Except for an occasional squawk, a pelican colony is silent! Nobody knows why.

Dive bomber

The brown pelican starts fishing while it is still flying above the water. It has such good eyesight that it can spot a fish from a hundred feet away. When it sees the fish it wants, the pelican folds its wings and dives into the water, headfirst, like a dart. It catches the fish with its beak and swallows it whole.

All for one and one for all

Pelicans love to do things together and to help each other. They swim together, eat together, and raise their young together. If one pelican is unable to fish, the other pelicans always bring their friend food.

Tell Me More

White pelicans have a particularly funny way of catching and eating their meals. They float together in a semicircle. Then, at exactly the same moment, they all dip their heads in the water to get a mouthful of fish.

Amazing but TRUE

The Seri Indians, who live on an island in the Gulf of California, figured out a way to get pelicans to do their fishing for them. They captured a pelican and kept it on the beach. The other pelicans brought back so many fish for the captured bird that there was enough food for the pelican and the Indians, too!

Why do some birds migrate?

In the fall, even before the ground starts to freeze, many birds fly to a warmer place to find food. They take the same route every year and go to the same place. In spring, when the weather gets warm, the birds return to where they came from. These yearly "round trips" are called *migrations*.

Some birds, like hummingbirds and falcons, migrate alone. But most birds fly in flocks. Geese, swans, and ducks fly together in flocks shaped like a giant V. Different birds take turns leading the way and the others follow in perfect formation.

Before the birds take off, their noisy chirps and honks seem to say: "The days are getting shorter. Winter is coming. Let's get going!" Then, all at once, they take off with a great flutter of wings.

Do all birds migrate?

Cardinals, blue jays, sparrows, mocking-birds, and some other birds stay near their nesting grounds all winter. When the cold weather comes, and they can't get their usual meal of worms and seeds, they nibble on acorns and dried berries.

Tell Me More

The golden plover travels from Alaska to Hawaii without stopping to rest!

Like squirrels, acorn woodpeckers spend the fall preparing for winter. They drill holes into trees, and then poke acorns into each hole. When winter comes, they have a nice big supply of food to eat!

Tell Me More

Though you have come to the last page of this book, you are only beginning to know about the wonderful true-life stories of birds. Scientists who study birds are called *ornithologists*. But you don't have to be an ornithologist to enjoy finding out more about these amazing members of the animal kingdom.

There seems to be a plan and a purpose for everything in nature. Large or small, beautiful or strange, each plant and animal has a role to fulfill. Each has an effect on something else that sooner or later has an effect on us.

Here are some more amazing-but-true facts to start you on your way to new discoveries:

• The bee hummingbird is the smallest of all birds. It is just two inches long. It can fly for five hundred miles without stopping, but it cannot walk.

• Migrating songbirds are having more and more trouble finding places where they can spend the winter. That's because trees are being cut down and houses are being built where the birds would otherwise gather. If these birds have no place to go, they will die and no songbird will ever be heard again.

• Starlings are great mimics. One day a man was standing alone on an empty football field. Suddenly, much to his surprise, he heard the roar of a crowd cheering its team on. But there was no one there—no one, that is, but a flock of starlings in a nearby tree. They must have been at the last football game, liked all the sounds they heard, and copied them!

• In ancient China, people attached tiny bamboo whistles to pigeons' tails. Each whistle played a different note. When the pigeons flew up into the sky, the people below were treated to a lovely concert.